Chris Bradford

BULLET CATCHER

BLOWBACK

With illustrations by
Nelson Evergreen

Barrington Stoke

For more information on Chris and his books visit:
www.chrisbradford.co.uk

First published in 2017 in Great Britain by
Barrington Stoke Ltd
18 Walker Street, Edinburgh, EH3 7LP

www.barringtonstoke.co.uk

Text © 2017 Chris Bradford
Illustrations © 2017 Nelson Evergreen

The moral right of Chris Bradford and Nelson Evergreen to be
identified as the author and illustrator of this work has been asserted
in accordance with the Copyright, Designs and Patents Act, 1988

A CIP catalogue record for this book is available
from the British Library upon request

ISBN: 978-1-78112-447-5

Printed in China by Leo

Warning: Do not attempt any of the techniques described within the book. These
can be highly dangerous and result in fatal injuries. The author and publisher take
no responsibility for any injuries resulting from attempting these techniques.

To Archie, Elizabeth, Magnus and Helen Caithness
A truly wonderful family

CONTENTS

CHAPTER 1
MESSENGER

The Near Future

Troy felt his skin frying to a crisp as blue arcs of electricity surged over him. His muscles jerked and twitched out of his control. The awful stench of his own burning hair filled his nostrils and his throat was sore from screaming.

Troy had never imagined he would die like this – at the hands of a teenage girl with a talent to conduct electricity at will. Bolts of lightning sparked from her fingertips and curled their jagged tendrils around Troy's helpless body as he flailed on the concrete floor of the subway platform.

"*Stop!*" Troy begged. "*Please stop!*"

To his surprise, she did. The killer current died as she dropped her hands. Troy groaned in relief and trembled as he lay on the dark platform. The girl stared at him with the cold interest of a snake eyeing its prey.

"Does it hurt?" she asked.

All Troy could do was give a feeble nod.

"Good," she said. Her pale face contorted in glee and her fingers crackled as she shot another flash of super-charged energy from her palms.

Troy was powerless to stop the attack. His own talent made him bulletproof, but he had no defence against a high-voltage shock. As the deadly electricity flooded through him, he screamed in agony. The pain ripped him apart from the inside, darkness filled his vision and his body fell limp.

"That's enough, Tricity!" The Judge ordered.

"But he isn't dead yet," Tricity said. She lowered her glowing white-hot hands. The purple tips of her jet-black hair still stood on end with static.

Troy drifted on the edge of passing out. He was all but dead as The Judge's black-and-white mask floated like a ghost before his eyes. With its smile and its tears, the Janus mask seemed to mock Troy's fate.

"We *don't* want to kill him," The Judge said.

To Troy, his gruff voice seemed to come from far away, like an echo in a cave.

Beside The Judge stood a boy with spiky hair and large coal-black eyes. He was Eagle Eye, the terrorist super-sniper Troy had followed into the subway. "Why shouldn't we kill him?" Eagle Eye asked.

"This bulletcatcher can be of use to us," The Judge explained. "He can be our messenger."

"Our messenger for what?" Tricity asked.

Troy *had* to hear their plan. He fought the pain, determined not to black out.

"Our divine mission is to purify Terminus City of the Council and all sinners," The Judge said. "Tricity, before you began this bulletcatcher's execution, I told him that we intend to kill Mayor Lomez and his daughter Pandora next."

"But aren't we –?" Eagle Eye began.

"Don't dare interrupt me!" The Judge back-handed him hard across the cheek.

Eagle Eye winced then bowed his head in apology.

The Judge carried on as if he'd done nothing to the boy. "When our messenger tells SPEAR of our plan, Medusa will send the bulletcatchers and the rest of her security force to the mayor's mansion. Once they are there, we can exterminate them all in one go."

The Judge looked up and clasped his hands together in prayer.

"And then our work will be done."

CHAPTER 2
ALL GONE

Troy jerked awake. He was soaked in sweat and panting hard. As he sat up in the narrow bed of the medical ward, Troy saw that the underground HQ of SPEAR – the secret close protection agency he worked for – was in darkness. There was only a soft green glow coming from the lights set into the floor. The ward was silent as death too. Just his heart-rate monitor beeping like an over-active video game.

Troy tried to calm himself.

But it had been no nightmare. What he was remembering was real.

Electrical burns still criss-crossed his body like the strikes of a whip and he felt as weak as a drained battery. But the horrific memory at least explained how he'd survived Tricity's attack. The Judge had *allowed* him to live.

Troy had been spared in order to deliver a message. One that put Pandora, her father and the entire Bulletcatcher team in grave danger.

It was a trap – and Troy was responsible for setting the trap.

He had to warn his friends.

Troy ripped the monitor pad off his chest, rolled out of bed and fell to the floor with a crash. His legs were too weak to stand. So he used the wall for support as he pulled himself to his feet and stumbled out of the ward. He staggered down the corridor into the huge round chamber of SPEAR's briefing room. The seats were all empty and the hologram desk at the centre was switched off.

"Medusa!" he called out into the gloom. "Lennox! Joe! Azumi!"

No one answered. Just the lonely echo of his own voice.

Troy worked his way around the upper gallery. The dining area was deserted. The Rec Room was locked. He checked each dorm room, but none of the beds had been slept in.

Troy headed for the gym. Their combat and fitness instructor Apollo often trained late. Troy thumbed the keypad and the door slid open. A robed figure stood in the darkness like a pale ghost.

Troy let out a startled cry before he realised who it was ... he hardly recognised himself in the mirror wall. In a white medical gown, his body looked skeletal and frail. His sandy hair was burned black at the tips, his face was thin and dark rings shadowed his eyes like bruises. It looked as if Tricity had shocked the life out of him.

Troy let the door slide shut and stumbled to the Reactor Room. But that was deserted too. As The Judge had predicted, the whole team must have gone to protect Pandora and Mayor Lomez from the terrorists.

Troy wiped the sweat from his brow and crossed the chamber to the Comms Room, where he collapsed into the control chair. He powered up the comms unit and pressed the talk button.

"Control to Medusa," he gasped into the mic. "Urgent message. Respond." He listened. But he got no answer from the speaker. Troy repeated his call. "Control to Medusa. Respond."

Still nothing. His fist closed around the mic as his panic grew.

"Joe! ... Azumi! ... Anyone?"

Nothing but the crackle of static ...

CHAPTER 3
BATTLE BOOSTER

Troy pulled off his medical gown and threw it on the floor of the ward. He grabbed the fresh clothes that had been left in a neat pile on the table by his bed. Somehow he had to get to the mayor's mansion.

As he fumbled to put on his T-shirt, a dull throb in his side reminded him of the sniper bullet. Troy inspected the large purple bruise and scabbed wound on his lower ribs. He was supposed to be bullet*proof*. That was why SPEAR had recruited him in the first place. But somehow the sniper's bullet had pierced his skin. It had stopped short of entering his body, but the wound raised alarming questions in his mind.

Had there been something special about the bullet itself? Or was his talent fading?

Troy swallowed hard, unnerved at the idea. He pulled down his T-shirt to cover the wound. Out of sight, out of mind. But still The Judge's words filled him with doubts. Was Medusa telling him the whole truth about his talent?

Troy pushed the question to the back of his mind. There were more urgent matters to deal with first. He still felt weak as he slipped on his shoes and jacket and stumbled out of the room. As he shuffled along to the ward exit, he heard the soft wheeze of a ventilator. Troy stopped and peered into the intensive care unit. There he saw a girl lying still and silent. Her skin was white as snow. Her hair platinum blonde. And the ice-blue eyes Troy knew so well were closed.

Kasia.

She was strapped to the bench of a Healer
Machine, with a mask over her mouth. A
sensor scanned her vital signs as a bio-laser
tended to the gunshot wound to her chest.

Troy entered the room and laid a hand on
her arm. Kasia's skin was cool to the touch.
'Cold as a corpse,' Troy thought, and his throat
tightened.

Kasia's talent was Reflex. She could react
six times faster than any other human. But
even she'd had no chance against a bullet
she couldn't see. Eagle Eye had shot her in
a blackout at the star-studded Concert for
Climate Change two days ago. At the time,
Kasia had saved Pandora from the sniper's
bullets, but now her own life hung in the
balance.

Tears stung Troy's eyes and he bowed his
head. The two of them hadn't always got on,
but the thought that Kasia didn't know ... might

never know ... how much he admired and liked her was too much to bear.

"She's stable," a soft voice said behind him.

Troy spun around. He was so used to hearing Apollo bellow combat instructions at him that he almost didn't recognise his voice when it was low and quiet. But the man's massive bulk was unmistakable. His shoulders barely fitted through the door leading from the inner office of the medical unit.

"What are you doing up?" Apollo asked. He gave Troy a sharp look.

"Medusa and the team are in serious danger and it's all my fault," Troy replied. Then he told Apollo what he'd remembered. "I tried to contact them," he finished, "but I got no response."

"That's because they've gone 'dark' to stop the Army of Freedom hacking into their comms," Apollo explained.

"But The Judge is planning an all-out attack," Troy said. "They won't be ready for it."

"Azumi will sense it coming," Apollo said with a confidence that took Troy by surprise.

"But even with her Blindsight talent she might not see the danger soon enough," Troy argued. "I have to warn them."

Troy lurched for the door, stumbled and knocked over a trolley of medical supplies.

Apollo grabbed his arm and pulled him back to his feet. "You're in no fit state to go anywhere."

"Then *you* go," Troy begged.

"No can do," Apollo said with a firm shake of his bald head. "Someone has to keep HQ secure, and monitor Kasia's condition. Listen, Medusa has an emergency communicator. If there's a serious problem, she'll let me know."

"What if she *can't* let you know?" Troy insisted. "I've seen what these terrorists are capable of. You haven't. They have stronger talents than us."

"Medusa is more than capable of handling anything they throw at her," Apollo said. His hand was still gripped tight on Troy's arm. "Plus, she has SPEAR's entire security force at the mansion. It's the terrorists who should be worried."

"You're wrong," Troy almost shouted in frustration. "I'm going whether you like it or not." Somehow he shook himself free of Apollo's grip and headed for the door again.

"WAIT!" Apollo barked.

"You can't stop me," Troy said. He tried to sound strong, but he knew Apollo could stop him no problem.

"You are one stubborn recruit," Apollo snarled. His lip curled as he glared at Troy.

Then he stepped over to a cabinet on the wall, unlocked it and removed a bottle from a glass shelf inside. He strode over to Troy.

Troy recoiled.

"In your condition," Apollo growled, "you'll need these to stand any chance against those terrorists."

Apollo twisted open the cap and shook two blue pills into Troy's hand.

"What are they?" Troy asked.

"Battle Boosters," Apollo replied. "Well, that's what we called them in the elite forces. The military designed them to help wounded soldiers survive a firefight. The pills block pain, prevent blood loss and power your body."

"Really?" Troy stared at the two pills. "They do all that?"

Apollo grinned. "They sure do. They make you super-charged. You'll feel like you can bust down walls, walk through fire and sprint like the wind. Well, at least for a few hours, and depending on how badly you've been hurt."

Troy grinned back at Apollo. "Here goes nothing," he said, and he swallowed the two pills in a flash. He took one last look at Kasia then headed for the door.

CHAPTER 4
FORTRESS

Troy took one of SPEAR's high-speed auto-drives to the mansion. When he got there he was relieved to find security in full force with armed guards patrolling the outer wall. As he approached the main gate, one of the guards blocked his path and ordered him to halt.

"I.D.," the guard demanded as three others aimed a lethal array of guns at Troy's head.

Troy took out his hologram pass and his I.D. was cleared. Two security hulks escorted him into the mansion.

"Troy!" Pandora cried as he entered the games room. "Oh Troy – you're OK!"

She almost knocked Troy over as she flung her arms around him. Her long black hair brushed against his cheek and for a moment Troy forgot all about the danger they were in. As a SPEAR recruit, Troy's task was to protect her – but Pandora was a girl like no other and he'd found himself falling in love with her. Not that he expected the glamorous daughter of the mayor to return his feelings.

"I heard you'd been ... *electrocuted?*" she said, staring at the red lines that criss-crossed his neck.

Troy nodded. "Subways can be dangerous places," he joked. He didn't want to alarm Pandora with the news that the terrorists had talents of their own.

"Good to see you on your feet," Lennox said. The brawny bulletcatcher strode over

and patted Troy on the back. Usually Troy was left reeling by one of his friend's back slaps. Lennox's Hercules gene made him 50% stronger than even the strongest weightlifter. But this time he hardly felt the impact. Apollo was right about those battle boosters!

"Shouldn't you be resting up?" Azumi said. She turned to face Troy from behind the sunglasses that covered her blind, milk-white eyes. She was sitting with Joe, who was playing a game of hologram chess against himself.

"I thought you might be missing me," Troy told her. He joined them both by the window. When he looked out, he spotted ranks of security guards patrolling the grounds.

Lennox laughed. "No chance of that! Not with a private cinema, laser bowling alley and Prism table. This mansion's got *everything*!" He swept an arm round to take in the mass of high-tech kit that filled the room.

"Your focus should be on Pandora, not games!" Troy snapped.

Lennox blinked at Troy's sudden outburst. "Don't worry, it is. But everything's fine."

"What about you?" Troy turned to Azumi. "Haven't you had *any* visions?"

"None," she said, then she whispered, "*Are you sure you're OK?*"

"I'm fine," Troy replied. His blood buzzed as if he'd drunk a dozen high-energy drinks. "In fact, I've never felt better."

"I'm sure you haven't," said Joe. He stopped his game of chess and squinted at Troy's face from behind his square-framed glasses. "Dilated pupils, flushed skin, raised pulse rate. It's obvious you're on –"

"Where's Medusa?" Troy cut in. Joe's keen observation skills were vital on a mission, but his autism talent meant that he always told it exactly like it was. And sometimes he noticed a little too much.

"She's with my father," Pandora said.

"I have to speak with them both right now," Troy said. "It's urgent."

Pandora led him out the room and down a long hall lined with marble and glittering with glass chandeliers. The other bulletcatchers followed in formation. Even in the apparent safety of the mansion their orders were to keep Pandora in view at all times.

They crossed the entrance hall with its dramatic curved staircase and huge modern art paintings, then they entered a library panelled in wood. Rows of priceless leather-bound books lined the walls and above the fireplace hung a portrait of a beautiful raven-haired woman with dark hazel eyes, high cheekbones and rosebud lips. The similarity to Pandora was striking.

"My mother," Pandora said, when she noticed the direction of Troy's gaze.

Troy knew from SPEAR's mission file that Pandora's mother had been killed by a terrorist bomb five years ago. And the tremble of Pandora's chin told him the loss was still raw for her. Troy could understand her pain. It had been only a year since his own parents had been murdered by the Army of Freedom in an attack on a shopping mall and his grief felt like a knife in his heart.

Pandora turned from the image of her mother to address the two bodyguards who stood by another door that led out of the library.

"I need to see my father," she said in a firm voice.

One of the bodyguards, a blond man with a neck of solid muscle, knocked on the door. A deep voice replied, "Enter."

Troy and the others followed Pandora into a drawing room. Mayor Lomez and Medusa were sitting in leather chairs looking out over the garden. The mayor was sipping from a brandy glass.

"*Hola, mi niña bonita,*" he said as he greeted his daughter with a warm smile. "What do you want, my darling?"

Troy stepped forward before Pandora had chance to reply. "Mayor Lomez, we're all in great danger," he said. "We have to leave right now –"

"Troy, what the hell are you doing here?" Medusa demanded. Her stone-grey eyes blazed as she stood up in anger. "I'm so sorry, Carlos, for the interruption but Troy is recovering from a serious injury and it seems he's in shock."

As Medusa began to usher Troy out of the room, she hissed at him. "You don't just barge into the mayor's mansion and alarm him like this."

"You have to listen to me," Troy insisted. "The Judge has used me to set up a trap."

Medusa came to a sharp stop at the door. "What?"

Troy told Medusa of The Judge's devious plan and her spiked white hair seemed to bristle in horror. She turned back to the mayor. "We must re-assess your security. If what Troy has told me is true, then you're not safe, even here."

Mayor Lomez waved away her concern. "We don't have to worry about the Army of Freedom here," he said, and he took another sip of his brandy. "Or The Judge ..."

He rose from his chair and waved them over to stand with him by the huge bay window. Outside, a sun terrace led to an oval swimming pool that reflected the cloudless blue sky like a mirror. Beyond the pool, immaculate gardens stretched into the distance, dotted with statues, fountains and tall trees. The huge grounds all ended in a high stone wall.

"As you well know, Medusa, the outer walls here are a metre thick and bomb-proof," the mayor said. "They're topped by an electric fence. Armed guards patrol the perimeter. CCTV cameras cover every inch of the grounds and guards are stationed in the garden. We have pressure sensors embedded in the grass to alert us to intruders. The doors are fitted with electronic keypads, locks and alarms. And the windows are made of the strongest ballistic glass. So." He smiled. "I don't think we need to worry. This mansion is more secure than any fortress."

"But it won't be enough to stop them," Troy said, thinking of the terrible powers the Army of Freedom had at its disposal.

Mayor Lomez laughed. "Not even Batman could break into this place!"

CHAPTER 5
JUDGEMENT DAY

"It's not Batman I'm afraid of," Troy said. "It's The Judge and his two talents. We're dealing with real-life villains here, not the comic book heroes I used to read about –"

A bolt of lightning struck a tree at the far end of the garden and made the lights in the mansion flicker.

"Where did *that* come from?" Pandora said. She peered up at the cloudless sky.

Azumi's face darkened. "Step away from the window!" she shouted.

Troy didn't need Azumi's blindsight to know what was about to happen. He grabbed Pandora and dived on top of her. A second later there was a loud bang as if a rock had hit the window. A round chip appeared on the outside of the glass – in a direct line with the mayor's head.

"See?" Mayor Lomez said. "Bulletproof glass." He put a finger to the window and tried to wipe the mark away. His reaction was calm, but a throbbing vein above his left temple gave away his unease.

"GET DOWN!" Troy cried. "It's the sniper, Eagle Eye."

Another bullet struck the window in the exact same spot. A crack appeared in the glass. Mayor Lomez flinched as a third bullet hit the mark. He backed away from the window as it began to break.

Troy heard a burst of radio chatter from Medusa's earpiece. She frowned then whispered into her throat mic. "Delta unit proceed to the main gate. We need back-up."

The mayor spun round. "Problems?" he asked.

Medusa shook her head. "Nothing my security forces can't handle."

More bolts of lightning shot up from behind the perimeter wall. The electric fence sparked along its length like a firecracker, then died.

Troy pulled Pandora to her feet. "We need to get out of here," he said. "Fast."

The mayor ran over to his desk and took out a tablet from the drawer. He tapped at the screen and a wall panel slid back to reveal a large video monitor. A grid of CCTV feeds from the mansion's cameras popped up. In all of them they could see the security forces firing upon gunmen in white masks with F4000 assault rifles.

"Army of Freedom fighters!" Lennox gasped.

It was clear from the guards' panic that they were outnumbered and losing the battle.

Joe pointed to a digital map of the mansion on the screen. A series of red dots blinked in the outer grounds. "Pressure sensors?" he asked.

The mayor nodded. "Triggered at the south end of the garden."

Lennox looked out of the window. "I don't see anyone ... apart from two guards."

Just then one of the guards dropped to the grass. A moment later his partner flew backwards as if he'd been kicked by a horse.

Joe's brow creased. "That's very interesting," he said.

"Interesting?" Lennox cried. "Weird and scary more like!"

They all watched in horror as a security guard sprinted towards the mansion – to be stopped in her tracks when a stone statue toppled from its plinth. She was crushed beneath its weight.

Pandora clasped Troy's hand. "What's going on?" she asked, her voice shaking.

"We're under attack," said Troy, "from The Judge's talents."

The two bodyguards who'd been guarding the drawing room burst in. "The outer defences have been breached!" the blond guard cried.

Gunmen in faceless white masks began to appear along the entire length of the garden wall.

"Enact Code Red protocol," Medusa ordered. "Evacuate the mayor and his daughter. Now."

As the two bodyguards strode over to escort the mayor out, a face appeared on the video feed from the main gate. It was a chilling black and white mask.

The Judge's smiling–crying face filled the screen. Then his rasping voice spoke.

"Judgement Day, Mayor Lomez."

CHAPTER 6
CODE RED

Troy bundled Pandora out of the drawing room. Lennox, Azumi and Joe ran alongside. In front, Medusa and the two bodyguards rushed Mayor Lomez down the hall towards the underground garage of the mansion.

Code Red protocol was SPEAR's emergency evacuation procedure. A bulletproof SUV was prepped at all times to speed the mayor and his daughter away to a secret safe house.

"This shouldn't be happening!" Mayor Lomez said. He sounded more angry than scared.

"I can only apologise," Medusa replied as she stopped and entered a code into a keypad. "But I promise to get you both to a safe place."

A hidden door slid open and Medusa led the way down two flights of stairs. At the bottom they went through another security door and entered the garage. The SUV was waiting for them, doors open, driver at the wheel, engine running.

"I've a bad vision about this," Azumi hissed.

"No surprise there!" Lennox said. His tone was sarcastic as the sound of distant gunfire boomed down the stairwell.

"We don't have much choice," Medusa said. "Let's move." She pushed the mayor ahead.

After a quick look around the deserted garage, Troy led Pandora past the mayor's long line of luxury sports cars and motorbikes. As they approached the SUV, a girl with black and purple hair stepped out from behind a gold Aston Martin.

"Watch out!" Troy cried. "It's Tricity." He pushed Pandora behind a jet black Lotus.

Bolts of white-blue light burst from Tricity's hands. The SUV lit up, its headlights exploded, its windscreen shattered and its tyres burst into flame. The driver inside jerked and screamed. In seconds the vehicle was a ball of fire.

"*What now?*" the mayor cried. He huddled in the shelter of a soft-top Ferrari with Medusa and the others.

"Do you have the key to any of these cars?" Joe asked.

"Upstairs in my office, with all the other keys," the mayor replied.

"That's no help to us," Joe said.

The mayor gritted his teeth and hissed at him. "You people advised me to keep them there for security reasons!"

The next target for Tricity's electrical storm was an orange Harley Davidson chopper. The bike's petrol tank ignited and an explosion rocked the garage.

"We can't stay here much longer," Medusa said as she shielded the mayor from the blast of heat.

"There's another SUV prepped in the driveway," the blond bodyguard said.

His partner, a dark-haired Hispanic woman, pulled out a snub-nosed machine gun from her jacket and fired at Tricity.

Tricity ducked behind a concrete pillar.

"GO!" the bodyguard said. "I'll cover you."

Bullets blasted the pillar as they sprinted back to the stairwell. They bounded up the stairs two at a time, and dashed into the mansion's grand entrance hall. Troy spotted a black SUV parked outside as the blond bodyguard scanned the gravel driveway. "Can't see any A.F. fighters," he said.

At that moment his partner burst from the stairwell. "Hurry!" she gasped, as she slammed the door behind her. "Electro-girl's trying to short-circuit the locks."

The blond bodyguard flung open the front door, checked the route was clear then waved to his partner – *Go!* Gun at the ready, the bodyguard had taken only two steps when a bullet shot her dead centre in the head. She crumpled to the ground and Pandora stifled a shocked cry with her hand.

"Eagle Eye!" Troy said. He tried to locate the sniper in the mansion grounds. "He never misses."

"It's fifty metres to the SUV," Joe said. "That's ten seconds out in the open. There's eight of us. Eagle Eye fired one round per second at the window. So none of us will survive."

"But Troy's bulletproof," Lennox pointed out.

"He can't protect all of us," said Medusa.

Troy nodded in agreement. Besides, he didn't fancy running a suicide mission to the vehicle. His talent ... *if it still worked* ... would stop a bullet or two. But ten bullets would push him beyond his limit, even pumped up on battle boosters.

Pandora's hazel eyes were wide with terror. "We're trapped then?" she said.

"Carlos, you have a safe room, don't you?" said Medusa.

The mayor nodded. "Yes, next to the master bedroom."

They turned and ran up the stairs. As they reached the landing, two gunmen in white masks kicked down the front door and fired up at them. Troy looked back and saw a short, round-faced boy behind the terrorists. His dark, snake-like eyes were fixed on Troy. Bullets pinged off the marble walls and ripped across priceless artworks. All of a sudden Troy felt a tap on his arm and there was a hole in his jacket. He'd been hit. But he felt zero pain.

"This way!" Mayor Lomez cried and he led them down a wide corridor. But before they could reach the master bedroom, the door slammed shut. Then a huge vase of flowers flew off a table and smashed the blond bodyguard over the head. He reeled from the blow.

"The door won't open." Medusa cursed as she yanked on the handle.

Lennox gave it a go. But he only succeeded in ripping the handle off.

"They're coming!" Azumi cried.

Lennox threw his body against the door again and again ... but each time he bounced off like a rubber ball. As he moved back for another try, a large mirror flew from the wall and struck him in the face. "What the hell?" he cried as blood streamed from a gash on his head.

"My room!" Pandora yelled. "We can get in that way."

They ran into her bedroom and crossed to an en-suite dressing room. Pandora put her thumb to a sensor pad and a full-length mirror slid back to reveal a steel door. The sound of pounding feet and angry shouts drew closer. The hidden door opened and they dived inside.

CHAPTER 7
SAFE ROOM

The safe room was designed for four people –
none of them the size of Lennox and the blond
bodyguard – so it was a little crowded as they
locked and bolted the steel door behind them.
A cubicle with a toilet and a shower took up
one corner. A small sink and cooking unit filled
another. A narrow bunk-bed was mounted on
one wall, and on the opposite side were shelves
of supplies and a small desk with a screen
above it.

The mayor sat in the only chair and keyed
a password onto the screen. Pandora perched
on the lower bunk with her head in her hands.
Troy put an arm around her to comfort her.

Azumi found the medical box and Joe helped her to dress Lennox's injury. Medusa and the blond bodyguard stood behind the mayor as the screen blinked to life to show a grid of security cameras.

A view of the underground garage showed the SUV still in flames.

"Why hasn't the fire sprinkler system kicked in?" the bodyguard asked.

"It's been shut down," the mayor said. He pointed to a flashing icon on the security app.

"Who by?" Medusa asked.

"The Judge or Tricity," Joe replied as he tied Lennox's bandage. "Water and electricity don't mix well. The terrorists wouldn't want to electrocute themselves by mistake."

Another video feed showed the main gate where all the mayor's security guards lay dead or dying.

"I don't believe this," Mayor Lomez muttered. The vein over his left temple throbbed. "It's –"

But he fell silent as a camera in the master bedroom showed a robed man enter and walk up to a tall mirror. Beside him stood Tricity and the snake-eyed boy Troy had spotted earlier. The figure looked up at the lens from behind his black and white mask.

"Knock, knock!" The Judge said, and he rapped on the mirror. "You can't hide from your sins, Mayor Lomez."

"I've no sins to hide," the mayor snapped into the mic on the screen. "Why are you here, Judge?"

"You know why I'm here," The Judge replied. "Unlock the door and we can discuss this like civilised men."

"Civilised?" Mayor Lomez spat. "Do you think I'm stupid?"

"No, I think you're guilty," The Judge said. "But first you must stand trial."

Mayor Lomez laughed. "You're the one who's guilty … and insane!"

Medusa spoke into the mic. "Judge, exit this property right now or –"

"Ah, Medusa!" The Judge cut in, his tone delighted. "You and I also have matters to discuss."

Shock flickered across Medusa's pale face as she realised that The Judge knew her voice. She swallowed hard then cleared her throat. "The police are on their way," she said. "They have orders to shoot to kill."

"I don't fear the police," The Judge said. "I don't fear you, Medusa. I fear no one … bar God. It is *you* who should tremble in fear and surrender up your souls. I have cut all comms. No one is coming to your rescue …"

As The Judge talked on, Azumi leaned close to Troy. "How many of us made it into this room?" she whispered.

Troy frowned. "Eight."

"Then why do I sense *nine* people in here?"

Troy looked around. He counted eight. The door to the toilet cubicle was ajar, but he couldn't see anyone else.

"... Now, open up the safe room or God have mercy on your souls," said The Judge.

"No – you leave now or I'll show *you* no mercy, Judge," Mayor Lomez replied. "Your reign of terror is over."

Now it was The Judge's turn to laugh. "My work ridding Terminus City of sin has barely begun," he said. "And from where I'm standing, you're in no position to make threats."

"The steel doors have an internal locking system – even your electro-girl can't short-circuit it," the mayor said. "We're protected by a metre of reinforced concrete, and we've our own air filtration system and supplies. Crawl back to your hell-hole, Judge. You won't *ever* get in."

"I wouldn't be so sure of that," The Judge said. He raised his hands to the camera like a wizard and called out, "Open Sesame!"

Troy and the others watched in horror as the door unlocked itself from the inside.

CHAPTER 8
THE TRIAL

"Let the trial begin," The Judge declared.

He struck the desk with a small wooden mallet and a sharp *crack* like a gunshot rang off the walls of the drawing room.

Troy's eyes darted around, looking for ways to escape or fight back. But they were surrounded on all sides. Two gunmen in white masks guarded the door. Another two stood by the bay window. Behind The Judge stood Tricity, Eagle Eye and two new talents. A girl with golden brown hair and sand-coloured skin. "Shifter," as the Mayor had called her when she'd suddenly appeared by the safe room door.

She'd been the invisible *ninth* person in the safe room – the one who had unlocked the door. Her talent was camouflage. Her skin was like a chameleon's, which explained the mystery of the two guards who had been knocked down in the garden by an unseen force.

The boy was silent and still as a cobra waiting to strike. His talent had yet to be revealed, but Troy had his suspicions.

"Will the accused step forward," The Judge said.

"This is a farce!" said Mayor Lomez. He ignored The Judge's request and the masked gunmen, and instead he strode over to the drinks cabinet and poured himself a large brandy. "You've taken your crusade too far, Judge."

Troy was stunned by the mayor's brazen nerve. Then he noticed him take a handgun from the cabinet and slip it into his belt under

his jumper. His courage was inspiring. 'No wonder he's the mayor of Terminus City,' Troy thought.

"Respect the court, Mayor," The Judge warned. "You are accused of deceit, fraud and murder."

Mayor Lomez downed his drink and laughed. "What sort of kangaroo court is this?" he demanded. "Those are the crimes *you're* guilty of, Judge."

"I'm not the one on trial," The Judge said. "You are."

The Judge nodded to a gunman and the mayor was forced back into line with Troy and the others.

"For those present," The Judge said, "let it be known that Mayor Lomez is the leader of the Army of Freedom. He's lied about the threat to Terminus City. He's held onto power by means of force and fear. And he is responsible for the deaths of the Council members and countless citizens –"

"These claims are outrageous," Medusa cut in. "What sort of fools do you take us f–"

"Silence, Medusa!" The Judge snapped. "Your trial is next."

Pandora stepped forward, as brave as her father. "My father would never do such things!" she yelled. "He's the elected mayor of the city. The people trust him to *destroy* the Army of Freedom, not to lead it."

"My dear girl, social control is best managed through fear," The Judge replied. "By inventing an external threat, people like your father can keep society off balance and paranoid. Dictators can then position themselves as the people's only hope. And thus they gain absolute power over them."

"Your accusations are unfounded," said Mayor Lomez. "No one will ever believe you!"

"Tricity, assist the mayor with his confession," The Judge ordered.

As Tricity pointed a sparking finger, Mayor Lomez glared at her. "Do your worst, but you won't get a word out of me," he said.

"Fine," Tricity said with a shrug. "Perhaps your daughter can persuade you to talk."

Before Troy could react, a bolt of electricity shot out and struck Pandora in the chest.

"No!" Troy cried. He dropped down with Lennox and Azumi to shield Pandora from further attack.

Tricity's hand crackled and glowed as an energy bolt charged up in her palm.

"STOP!" Mayor Lomez shouted, his face red with anger. "You're under *my* command!"

"Not any more," The Judge replied. He held up a hand for Tricity to stop. "But thank you for your confession."

Medusa, Troy and the others stared in disbelief at the mayor.

"Father?" Pandora gasped, as tears of pain and shock welled up in her eyes.

"I–I–I meant *I'm* in charge ... I'm the mayor," he stuttered. He turned away from his daughter's gaze.

"Your immoral plan has turned in on itself," The Judge went on. "You used me as a weapon to strike fear into the citizens of this city. Now that weapon is pointing back at you. This is what spies call *blowback*."

The Judge struck his mallet on the table.

"Mayor Lomez, you're guilty as charged. I sentence you to death."

CHAPTER 9
EXECUTION

"This can't be true," Troy said as The Judge laid a handgun on the table. "Your terrorists targeted Pandora. Why would Mayor Lomez want to kill his own daughter?"

The Judge's black and white mask turned towards Troy. "Mayor Lomez made Pandora appear to be a target, so he could create more fear among the people, demand more power from the Council, and keep any suspicion away from himself. In the subway I told you to question who you protect and why. Remember? I'm just the weapon. Mayor Lomez is the one who pulls the trigger."

Troy looked to the mayor for a denial, but the truth was written all over his pale face. Troy realised that *this* was the man responsible for his parents' murder.

The Judge cocked his gun and aimed it at the mayor. "As judge, jury and executioner ..."

Mayor Lomez looked to his blond bodyguard. "For heaven's sake, protect me!"

The bodyguard shook his head and backed away.

"It seems, Mayor, that you're losing your grip on power," The Judge said. He shot the bodyguard between the eyes.

Unprotected, Mayor Lomez now seized Troy and held him in front of him as a shield. From his belt, he pulled out the hidden handgun and fired at The Judge.

The shot was at point-blank range, but the bullet simply shattered a mirror behind

The Judge. Then the gun flew from the mayor's grip and ended up in the hands of the strange snake-eyed boy.

"Had you forgotten that Feng's talent is telekinesis?" The Judge said. "He can move objects with his mind."

Troy's suspicions had been right – the boy's talent explained toppling statues, closing bedroom doors and flying ornaments.

"Unfortunately, Mayor, the bulletcatcher you're holding is losing *his* talent," The Judge said with a cruel laugh. "He's no longer bulletproof."

The Judge fired.

Troy felt the bullet's impact as it passed right through his shoulder. Again there was no pain – but the mayor screamed and the two of them fell to the floor. Pandora rushed to her father's side as blood poured from a gaping wound in his chest.

"I'm sorry ... *mi niña bonita*," her father groaned. "I only wanted to keep you safe ... Terminus City safe ... After your mother's death, I vowed to take absolute control ... to stop it ever happening again ... it was a choice between safety and freedom ... can't have both ..."

Mayor Lomez's eyes glazed over. Pandora hugged her dead father's body, as tears poured down her face.

Lennox tried to sit Troy up. "Troy! Are you all right?" he asked.

Troy nodded. He examined the second hole in his jacket. There was no blood, but he knew it wasn't his talent that had saved him. It was the battle boosters – and he dreaded what would happen when their powers wore off.

"You're the devil incarnate!" Medusa spat, and her stone-grey eyes burned at The Judge. "How can you justify shooting this boy to kill the mayor?"

"I'm not the one who put him in the line of fire," The Judge replied. "That was you, Medusa." He paused. "By the way, did you inform your recruits that their talents can fail? No, I didn't think so. As I told you, Troy, Medusa wasn't telling the whole truth. All she cares about is SPEAR. She doesn't care that she's risking your lives."

Troy looked to Medusa. Her grey eyes were wide and she was shaking her head.

"Don't listen to him," she begged. "You know that *you* are my priority."

"And did you tell them about your *own* talent for mind control?" The Judge asked.

Troy swapped stunned looks with Lennox and the others.

"That explains a lot," Joe said, in a matter-of-fact tone.

"Her powers have become weak over time," The Judge admitted, "yet they are still strong enough to influence the thinking of a vulnerable child."

"He's lying!" Medusa cried, but Troy recalled the stone-grey eyes that had filled his vision that day in the hospital. *"Join SPEAR. It's your best hope*," she had said and the decision was made for him.

"Your trial is at an end, Medusa," The Judge said. "The verdict is in."

As he aimed his gun, Medusa snarled, "And when is your trial, Judge?"

"My time will come," he declared. "Everybody has their Judgement Day."

And he pulled the trigger.

CHAPTER 10
BACK FROM THE DEAD

In the nano-second before The Judge's gun fired its bullets, Azumi warned Troy and the others, "Close your eyes! Cover your ears!"

A moment later the bay window exploded in a hailstorm of glass. The two terrorist guards were blown off their feet and The Judge was knocked back into his chair. His aim was thrown off, and the bullet meant for Medusa's heart clipped the side of her head instead. Dazed, she dropped to her knees as blood streamed down her face. Then a stun grenade clattered across the floor. There was a lightning white flash and a bang like a thunder clap.

Despite Azumi's warning, Troy's ears still rang. But he wasn't stunned or blinded like The Judge and his talents. Through the smoke, Troy saw the doors to the drawing room fly open and a guardian angel appeared ...

Kasia!

In the blink of an eye, she disarmed both remaining guards then knocked them out with the butt of their guns. A moment later Apollo strode in from the shattered window carrying the largest assault rifle Troy had ever seen in his life.

"You got my message then?" Medusa groaned as Apollo lifted her up and put her back on her feet.

"Loud and clear," Apollo replied.

"Kasia, you're OK!" Troy said, standing up to greet her.

"Back from the dead." She grinned and Troy knew from the sparkle in her ice-blue eyes that she was on battle boosters too.

"Let's move!" Apollo barked as another wave of gunmen in white masks surged across the mansion grounds towards them.

Troy dragged the sobbing Pandora off her father's dead body. "He's gone, for good," he told her, without a shred of pity for the man. "But you're not ... and I've sworn to protect you."

They dashed out onto the sun terrace after the others. Apollo's rifle thundered and masked gunmen dropped like nine-pins in a bowling alley. Those who survived Apollo's attack took cover and returned fire, every bit as fierce.

"We're cut off from our escape vehicle," Kasia said as they sheltered behind the pillars by the swimming pool.

"What about the SUV out front?" Joe reminded them.

"Good thinking," said Medusa. "Apollo, cover us."

The assault rifle roared again. Joe was leading the way when his head rocked back and he spat blood. Another invisible blow doubled him over.

"It's Shifter!" Troy cried.

"Where is she? I can't see her," Lennox said. He stepped to Joe's defence and raised his beefy fists.

"Don't worry, I can sense her," Azumi said, and she launched a perfect side kick into thin air.

There was a grunt and for a brief second a pair of dark brown eyes shimmered before them ... then vanished.

"You can't hide from me," Azumi said as she fought the air. Her strong legs whirled and her fists flew.

"Come on," Medusa yelled. "To the SU–"

A huge bolt of electricity blasted her backwards.

"Not so fast!" Tricity yelled as she strode out of the drawing room. A twin high-voltage beam shot from her palms. Troy shielded Pandora with his body and he got the full force of the strike. The battle boosters meant he didn't suffer the excruciating pain he had before, but he still felt each and every muscle spasm as he thrashed on the floor, unable to save himself.

Lennox rushed at Tricity. She turned on him. Lightning coursed over his body but it didn't stop him. He charged into her like a steel battering ram. She went down and they tumbled head over heels into the garden.

When Troy's muscles stopped their violent twitching, he became aware of someone shaking his arm. Pandora was staring down at him, her eyes wet with fresh tears. "Troy! Troy!"

"I'm good," he said, realising her tears were for him. He got back to his feet and scanned the battle scene.

Joe had recovered from Shifter's sneak attack and was putting his glasses back straight. Beside him Medusa's body twitched but she showed no other signs of life. Apollo was still keeping the masked gunmen at bay. His rifle blasted away, but he was running out of bullets fast. Then the pillar he was crouched behind began to topple over.

"Apollo!" Troy shouted. "Watch out!"

Apollo rolled to one side as the stone pillar came crashing down. It shattered into a hundred pieces. Then one jagged lump lifted off the ground and flew at Kasia's head. She ducked as her Reflex talent saved her from the fatal blow.

"That's Feng again," Troy cried. He pointed to the dark-haired boy standing by the broken bay window, his snake-like eyes narrowed in focus.

"You get Pandora to safety!" Kasia ordered as she dodged another chunk of stone. "We can handle these talents."

CHAPTER 11
LINE OF FIRE

Troy rushed Pandora along the path to the far end of the mansion. The SUV was still parked in the gravel drive. He looked back. His friends were locked in battle with Tricity, Feng and Shifter. Apollo was down to his last clip of ammo. Troy wondered if he should be deserting them at all. Then a bullet pinged off the brick wall of the mansion, close to Pandora's head.

On instinct Troy leaped into the line of fire. A second bullet bounced off the wings of a stone angel statue, a good metre from where they stood. Troy heard someone curse and

Eagle Eye the sniper stepped out from behind a bush. His rifle was aimed at Pandora.

Troy was stunned. "I thought you never missed," he shouted.

"I don't!" Eagle Eye snapped, coming closer to get a better shot. The boy was blinking over and over as tears streamed from his large round eyes. Troy realised the stun grenade had done Eagle Eye more damage than anyone else.

As the sniper wiped his watery eyes, Joe ran up behind him and kicked his legs from under him. "Go!" Joe shouted to Troy as he wrestled the rifle from Eagle Eye.

Troy grabbed Pandora's hand and dashed across to the SUV. He flung open the driver's door and they jumped in ... but they couldn't start the car.

"You'll be needing this," a rasping voice said.

The masked face of The Judge leered at them from the other side of the window. He held a sleek black key fob in one hand. In the other was a gun.

"Get out!" he ordered with a wave of the gun.

Troy shielded Pandora as they stood before The Judge.

"Is she *really* worth protecting?" The Judge asked. He aimed his barrel at Troy and Pandora. "Are you ready to lay down your life for the daughter of the man responsible for your parents' murder?"

"Whatever her father did, Pandora is innocent," Troy said. "You're the one with blood on your hands."

"Pandora bears the sins of her father," The Judge spat. "She can't be allowed to live." His finger curled round the trigger. "Last chance ..."

Troy stood his ground between The Judge and Pandora.

The moment the bullet struck his chest, he shoved Pandora aside, out of the line of fire. "RUN!" he yelled.

As Troy slumped to the ground, he watched Pandora sprint up the drive. His chest burned where the bullet had hit him and he knew the battle boosters were wearing off.

The Judge stood over him as he reloaded his gun. "A heroic sacrifice, Troy," he said, "but you've only delayed her judgement."

The Judge took slow, careful aim at Pandora as she ran and shot her in the back.

CHAPTER 12
DIVINE JUSTICE

"NOOOOO!" Troy screamed as Pandora stumbled then tried to stagger on a few more steps.

The Judge fired again and she fell face first into the dirt.

"YOU DEMON!" Troy bawled. "YOU FACELESS FREAK!"

"Careful what you say, Troy," The Judge said, his voice as cold as ever, "or you'll find yourself on trial again."

"Your trials aren't real trials!" Troy spat. "They're excuses for murder!"

"I am the angel of death," The Judge declared. "I've been sent to cleanse this city of sin – and so I will."

The wound in Troy's chest was agony and blood was seeping out of the holes in his jacket. He could see his friends still bravely battling the talents. But Apollo had run out of ammo and been shot in the leg. He was trying to drag Medusa to safety. Azumi's glasses were smashed and her mouth was bleeding, and it was clear she was losing the fight with Shifter – the ghost girl only visible when Azumi landed an occasional punch or a kick. Joe was pinned to the ground by Eagle Eye, who had his rifle pressed up against Joe's throat. Lennox had Tricity in his powerful grip. Arcs of electricity flowed down his back like a cape. He was roaring in pain and rage yet somehow he was able to stand up to her attack. *But for how much longer?*

Then Troy saw Kasia sprint up the path. She weaved and dodged as bricks, stones and chunks of broken pillar flew at her. When she spotted Troy at The Judge's feet, she ground to a sudden halt beside the angel statue. Her look was one of shock and dismay. Then she turned back to the battle and shouted in fury, "Is that all you can manage, Feng? Pebbles and rocks?"

More missiles flew at her as she ran onto the drive.

Troy knew they were defeated. He glared up at the black and white mask of The Judge. "You're no angel," he said bitterly. "You're a devil. That's why you hide behind a two-faced mask."

"I'll tell you the reason I wear this Janus mask," The Judge said. "Janus is the Roman god of all beginnings. He presides over the start and end of any conflict. The doors of his temple open in time of war and close to mark the coming of peace. Under my rule, there'll be a new beginning as I bring true peace to Terminus City."

The Judge aimed his gun at Troy's head.

"But first, I must cleanse the city of you and your bulletcatchers," he said.

Troy had no strength to fight back. As the battle boosters faded into nothing, the pain bloomed and his lifeblood flowed out.

He was no longer bulletproof, and he braced himself for the killing shot.

Then out of the sky flew an angel. It crushed The Judge and he crumpled into the gravel next to Troy. His black and white mask wept tears of blood.

CHAPTER 13
HIDDEN TALENT

"That was close!" Kasia said as she sank to her knees beside Troy. "I almost didn't get out of the way in time."

Troy stared at the stone angel that Feng had launched at Kasia just as she crept up behind The Judge. "I guess that's what you call divine justice," he said with a grim smile.

He heard a crunch of gravel as Feng appeared. The boy froze when he saw The Judge lying dead beneath the angel. For a moment Troy thought Feng might raise it up and crush him and Kasia with it. But Feng was horrified at his fatal mistake. He backed away and shouted to the other talents, "The Judge is dead!"

Now that his master no longer held the balance of power, Feng bolted and disappeared into the trees.

"So much for The Judge's loyal followers," Kasia said. She helped Troy to sit up. His chest burned like fire and his shirt was soaked with blood.

"We need to get you to a hospital," Kasia said, and she grabbed the key fob from The Judge's limp hand.

"What about the others?" Troy wheezed.

Kasia looked over her shoulder. "They're just tidying up the mess," she said with a grin.

Azumi had leaped into the air and was in the middle of a devastating spinning kick. A second later a body shimmered into view at her feet. Her heel had caught Shifter's invisible jaw and the girl had been knocked out cold.

Lennox was lit up like a lightbulb. Streaks of electricity were raining down on him as he lifted the furious Tricity above his head. Then, with a mighty effort, he tossed her into the swimming pool. There was a massive explosive spark followed by a hiss of steam. When the air cleared, Tricity's charred body could be seen floating in the water.

"You were right, Joe," Lennox called out. His curls of black hair were smoking. "Water and electricity don't mix!"

But Joe wasn't in such a winning position as the others. He'd managed to throw Eagle Eye off, only for the sniper to turn his rifle on him. Yet Joe appeared unfazed as Eagle Eye aimed the weapon and pulled the trigger ...

Click ... click ... click.

"You'll be needing these," Joe said. He opened his hand to reveal the bullets he'd taken from the gun during their struggle.

"Give them back!" Eagle Eye snarled.

"Of course," Joe said and he tossed the bullets at Eagle Eye's feet.

As he scrabbled on the ground to reload, Eagle Eye never knew what hit him. Lennox strode up behind him and struck the boy on the head like a sledge hammer driving a post into the ground.

"It always amazes me," Joe said, "how easy it is to distract the eye."

Apollo, limping badly, appeared with Medusa slung over his back. "The Judge's gunmen are in retreat," he grunted as he lowered Medusa into the back seat of the SUV. "But when they realise we're out of ammo, they might return to finish us off."

Now their opponents were dispatched, Lennox, Joe and Azumi sprinted across the drive to join them in the SUV.

"Let's go," Apollo ordered, and he herded them into the vehicle.

"But what about Pandora?" said Troy. He staggered over and sank down by her lifeless body. He brushed a lock of raven hair from her angel face. Troy loved this girl. He'd been willing to die for her. Yet that hadn't been enough.

"We're too late to save her," Apollo said, laying a hand on him, "but *you* need urgent medical attention. Come on."

"We can't give up on her."

"Troy, you took a bullet for her – several by the looks of it. No one could ask you to do more. But we have to go. Now."

Troy no longer had the strength to stand. As Apollo lifted him into his arms, Troy thought he saw Pandora's eyes flicker.

"Wait!" he said. "She's alive."

"Don't fool yourself," Apollo said as he carried Troy to the SUV. "Only a bulletcatcher like you could survive two rounds in the back."

CHAPTER 14
FREE CHOICE

"I cut my knee open once falling off my bike. By the time I'd limped home and told my mother, it was healed. I always thought I was just lucky." Pandora laughed. "Who knew I had a talent for self-healing?"

Troy listened in amazement as he lay on the narrow bed in SPEAR's medical ward. A Healer Machine hummed beside him, its bio-lasers tending to his gunshot wounds. Pandora sat next to him, holding his hand. For Troy that was the most wonderful feeling in the world. Second only to seeing Pandora come back to life and sit up on the gravel of the mansion's drive.

"So you never needed us to protect you at all!" Kasia said with a roll of her eyes. She lay in the bed next to Troy's, attached to her own Healer Machine.

"I wouldn't say that," Pandora replied, giving Troy's hand a squeeze.

"Well, who'd have thought I had a *double* talent?" Lennox said. He thrust out his broad chest. "I'm shockproof!"

"That's not technically true," Joe said as he cleaned his glasses with his T-shirt. "You just have a higher resistance due to your bulk."

Lennox frowned. "Are you saying I'm *fat*?"

"He's saying you're lucky too," Azumi said, sucking at her swollen lower lip.

Troy winced as the Healer Machine laser-stitched his skin. "Well, I wish I had a self-healing talent," he said.

"We could always take a battle booster," Kasia said with a wink.

"No more battle boosters for you two!" Apollo growled from the inner office. "Drugs are never the answer. You both need time to heal properly."

Medusa walked stiffly into the ward. Her white hair was styled in its usual spikes but now it made her appear like she was still being electrocuted.

"I've good news," she announced. "The Army of Freedom has disbanded following news of The Judge's death. His talents have vanished too. It seems The Judge ruled with an iron fist and no one has stepped forward to take his place."

"What about the Council?" Azumi asked. "Who's going to run the city now?"

"There's only one surviving Council member and she is no fit state to rule. She's proposed that Pandora governs the city."

Pandora's mouth fell open. "Me?" she exclaimed.

Medusa nodded. "You're the people's choice. For the sake of law and order, we've not disclosed your father's links with the terrorists. And we know you had nothing to do with it."

Pandora hung her head and sighed. "My father may have been wrong in his methods, but his reasons were good."

After a minute's silence, she looked up with a steely glint in her hazel eyes. "We need to make Terminus City safe," she said. "But the price cannot be freedom. Peace in the shadow of fear is not peace. We have to have the choice to live free."

"You're going to make a fine mayor," Medusa said with a rare smile. "And SPEAR will continue to protect you. That's if my bulletcatchers wish to stay?"

Medusa turned to Troy and the others, with a pained look on her pale face.

"I can only apologise for using my talent to influence you," she said. "There are so few of you in the world ... When I met a talent capable and worthy of being a bulletcatcher, I did anything in my power to recruit them."

Medusa bowed her head in shame, fixing her eyes on the floor. "I'll understand if you want to leave," she said. "As Pandora said, you have the choice to live free."

Troy and the others exchanged looks but said nothing.

Then Joe spoke up. "The question is, if we had known then what we know now, would we have made a different choice?"

Troy thought back to that moment in hospital. Alone, orphaned and scared. *Would he have made a different choice?*

"There was never any doubt in my mind," Kasia said. "I'm still in."

"We're a team, aren't we?" Lennox grinned. "I'm staying if you're staying."

Joe nodded. "This is where I belong. My autism is my strength at SPEAR."

"And my Blindsight has purpose," Azumi agreed. "Besides, I stick by my friends."

"What about you, Troy?" Kasia asked. "Without your talent, you've only got your training to rely on."

"I may not be able to catch bullets any more," Troy said, smiling at her and the rest of the team, "but I'll *always* be a bulletcatcher."

Our books are tested
for children and young people by
children and young people.

Thanks to everyone who consulted on
a manuscript for their time and effort in
helping us to make our books better
for our readers.

BULLET CATCHER

BLOWBACK